First sleepover

Story by Carole Mohr

Illustrations by Mark Weber

Dr. Judith Nadell, Series Editor

Kendra and Layla were going to sleep at Aunt Tonya's house.

This was Layla's first sleepover.

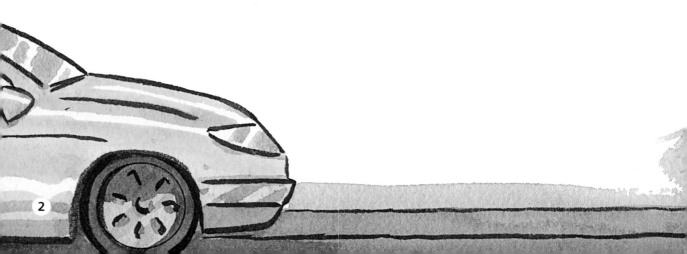

Kendra and Layla had fun at the sleepover.

They played games.

They played dress-up.

They read a good book.

Soon it was time for bed.

Aunt Tonya said, "Good night, girls."

She turned off the light and closed the door.

But Layla had a problem.

"The room is too dark," she said.

"I am scared.

I want to go home."

"Don't be scared," said Kendra.

"I am here.

We are together."

Layla closed her eyes.

Kendra went back to her bed.

"Don't go," said Layla.

"We are **not** together.

I am here, and you are there.

I am scared."

Now **Kendra** had a problem, too.

She was tired and wanted to go to sleep.

She thought of a way to fix her problem and Layla's.

Now Layla was not scared.

She could go to sleep.

So could Kendra.